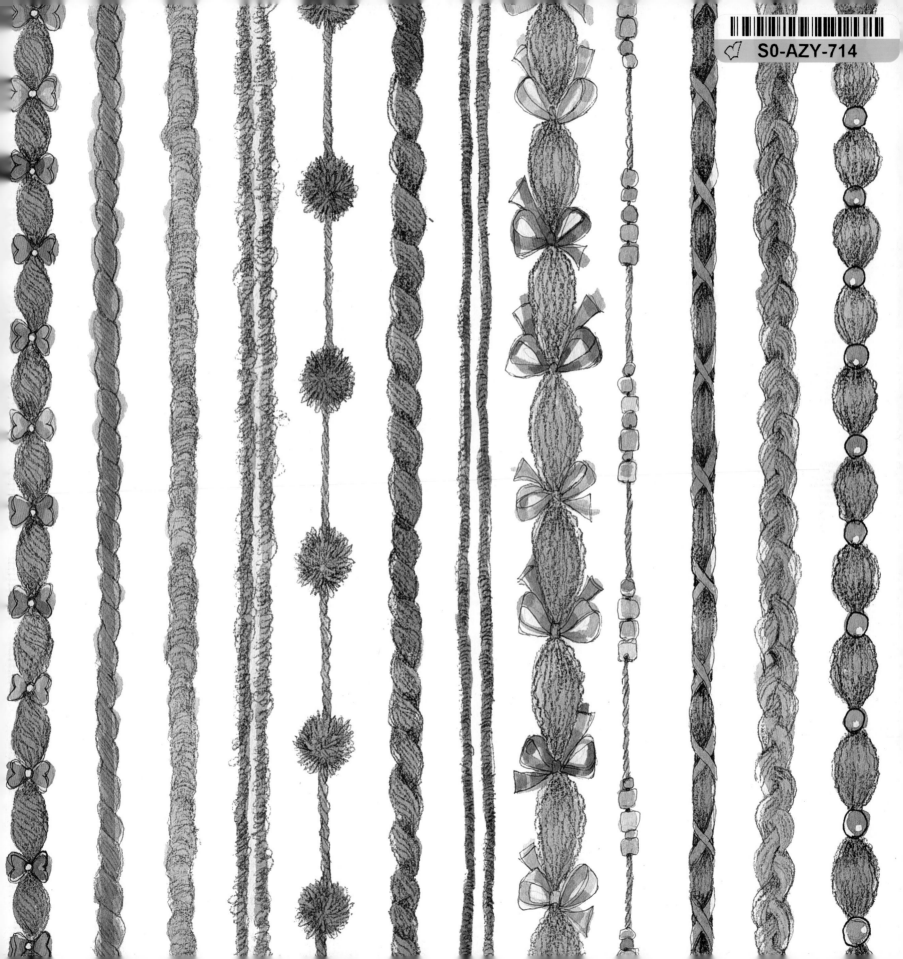

To all children who graciously donate their hair. You are loved.

All rights reserved. Published in the United States by Crown Books for Young Readers, an imprint of
Random House Children's Books, a division of Penguin Random House LLC, New York.

Crown and the colophon are registered trademarks of Penguin Random House LLC.

Visit us on the Web! rhcbooks.com

Educators and librarians, for a variety of teaching tools, visit us at RHTeachersLibrarians.com

Library of Congress Cataloging-in-Publication Data is available upon request.
ISBN 978-0-593-42688-3 (hardcover) — ISBN 978-0-593-42690-6 (ebook) — ISBN 978-0-593-57078-4 (lib. bdg.)

The artist used watercolor to create the illustrations for this book.
The text of this book is set in 18-point New Century Schoolbook.
Interior design by Jan Gerardi

MANUFACTURED IN CHINA
10 9 8 7 6 5 4 3 2 1
First Edition

Hair to Share

by Sylvia Walker

Crown Books for Young Readers

New York

Suri was born with more hair than anyone had ever seen on a baby.

As she grew . . .

. . . so did her hair.

Suri loved the special
ways Mom styled it.

At school, she was proud to show
her friends all her favorite styles.

One day at the park, Suri noticed a girl wearing the most spectacular scarf. It was covered in flowers, with a silky purple trim. It reminded Suri of a field of lavender.

"Hey! My name's Suri. I really like your scarf. Purple is my favorite color!"

"I'm Amaya, and purple's MY favorite color TOO!"

Suri's hair reminded Amaya of shooting stars in the night sky.

Suri and Amaya met
every day at the park . . .

played together . . .

. . . and soon became best friends.

Then one day, while she was turning cartwheels on the grass,
Amaya's purple scarf flew off and blew away in the wind.
Suri was surprised to see that Amaya didn't have any hair.

Suri grabbed the scarf, but when
she turned around, she realized that
Amaya had run off.

"Please come back!" called Suri,
but her friend was already gone.

Every day Suri searched the park . . .

. . . and the neighborhood.
She showed the purple scarf to
everyone, but no one recognized it.

Suri and her mom talked again about what had happened with her new friend. "Do you think Amaya didn't want me to see her without her scarf?"

"There are lots of reasons someone might not have hair. Even though they are still beautiful inside and out, wearing something pretty on their head can make them feel more comfortable and confident."

"Oh, I don't want Amaya to feel sad without her scarf. It's her favorite color. . . . Do you think I'll ever see her again? I wish I could give her some of my hair."

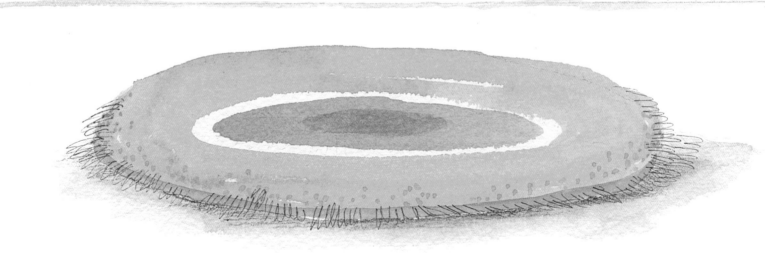

The next day, Suri and Mom decided to
search the neighborhood one more time.
As they passed the art supply store . . .

. . . Suri noticed a sign on a hair salon window.
Maybe this was just the solution to bring her
friend Amaya back!

"I want to donate! I want to donate!
I have more than enough hair!" exclaimed
Suri as she skipped through the door.

She showed the stylist the beautiful purple scarf.
The stylist recognized the scarf and knew exactly who it
belonged to. "Amaya is on our waiting list to receive a wig!"
she announced gleefully. Now Suri could donate her hair
for her friend.

Suri's hair was . . .

washed,

cut,

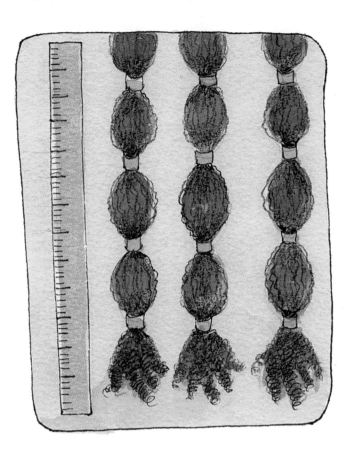

measured,

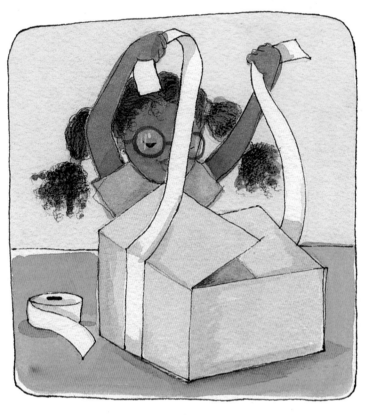

wrapped,

and mailed.

All summer long, Suri watched for Amaya and wondered, "Will she like the wig? Will she be surprised? Will she know it's from me?"

One morning, Suri sat on a swing, looking at the purple scarf and feeling sad. She missed her friend. Amaya wasn't swinging with her anymore.

Then, suddenly, she noticed someone walking toward her. . . .

Suri couldn't believe her eyes as Amaya stood before her. She recognized the hair she had shared.

"You got it! You got it!"

"Thank you! Thank you!" said Amaya. She was overjoyed
and feeling a boost of confidence, knowing her new best friend
had chosen to share her glorious, awesome hair with her.

"You're welcome," giggled Suri. "I kept your scarf, hoping
you'd come back."

Amaya had a surprise for Suri! "I want you to have this!"
She tied the beautiful purple scarf onto Suri's head. "It's
your favorite color, and now it's MY turn to share."

Why We Share Our Hair

There are many reasons why kids may experience long-term hair loss. Some may be living with alopecia areata, which causes the hair follicles to shrink and stop growing hair. Others may be battling cancer and struggling with hair loss caused by radiation therapy and chemotherapy.

Kids like Amaya who receive hairpieces often feel they've lost more than their hair; they can have a hard time feeling like themselves. Many kids have been teased or bullied for looking a bit different, and they can be embarrassed by the attention they receive because of their hair loss. Wearing a hairpiece can help kids dealing with hair loss feel like they fit in.

If you would like to help a kid find joy, just as Suri did for Amaya, talk to an adult about making a hair donation! Together, you can follow these easy steps to make a big difference in someone's life.

- Your hair should be ten inches or longer.
- Find a participating salon in your area, or have a grown-up help you at home.
- Make a ponytail with a rubber band, tying off the ten or more inches of hair.
- Have a grown-up cut the hair just above the rubber band.
- Put the ponytail in a plastic bag, and seal it tight.
- Put the plastic bag inside a large mailing envelope.
- Mail your donated hair at a post office.

If you would like to receive a hair donation,
these nonprofit charities may be able to help:

LOCKS OF LOVE
CHILDREN WITH HAIR LOSS
HAIR WE SHARE
LITTLE PRINCESS TRUST

And most important of all: celebrate your friends
for the beauty they share with the world!

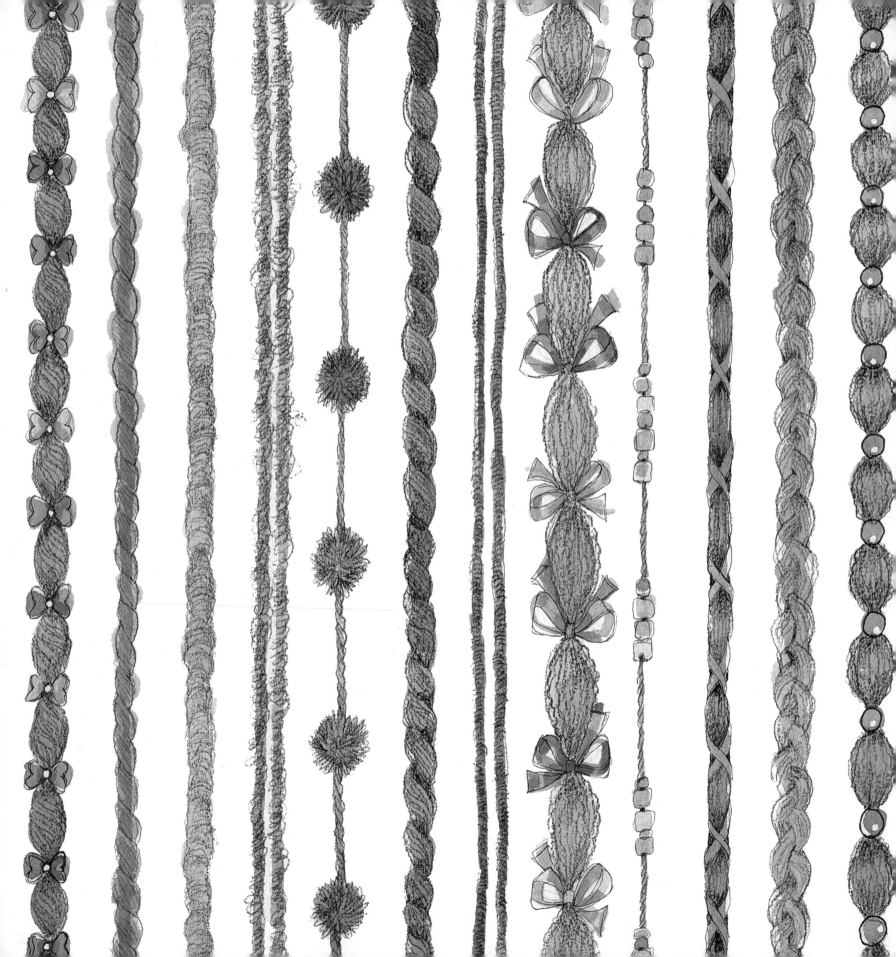